WINNING THE RANCHER'S HEART

HISTORICAL WESTERN ROMANCE

THE BACHELOR'S OF MOONBEAM RANCH
BOOK FIVE

TERRI GRACE

PUREREAD.COM

Copyright © 2025 PureRead Ltd

www.pureread.com

All rights reserved. No part of this publication may be reproduced, distributed or transmitted in any form or by any means, without prior written permission.

Publisher's Note: This is a work of fiction. Names, characters, places, and incidents are a product of the author's imagination. Locales and public names are sometimes used for atmospheric purposes. Any resemblance to actual people, living or dead, or to businesses, companies, events, institutions, or locales is completely coincidental.

CONTENTS

Dear reader, get ready for another great story...	1
Prologue	3
1. A New Home	7
2. Dismal Thoughts	17
3. The Pursuit of Happiness	33
4. Knowing Her Place	42
5. Trials and Tribulations	49
6. Here Comes Trouble	64
7. She Doesn't Belong	72
8. Don't Touch My Love	76
9. Marching Orders	84
10. The Girl Is Mine	93
Other Books In This Series	97
Our Gift To You	99

DEAR READER, GET READY FOR ANOTHER GREAT STORY...

A CHRISTIAN WESTERN ROMANCE

Turn the page and let's begin

PROLOGUE

"You'll never amount to anything because you're just as foolish as your mother was," Aunt Lena's voice rang in twenty-eight-year-old Charlotte Beamer's thoughts. "I'm doing you a great favor by even having you in my home, and you should be contented with your lot."

Charlie's lips tightened as she fought the despair that threatened to overwhelm her. This was her second month in Beaverhead, and she loved it here. Though there was much work to be done in the large ranch house, at least she got paid for her services. For the first time in her life, Charlie had money of her own, and each week as she watched her savings grow, she thanked the Lord for giving her this chance in life. She barely touched her wages because everything was provided for her by her cousin who was now married to one of the masters of this home.

Her life right now was unlike how it had been at Aunt Lena's house, where she'd lived for the past twenty years. Aunt Lena was her mother's younger sister but had treated her as if she was lower than the servants in her household. According to Aunt Lena, providing a roof over her head and basic food was enough, and Charlie should be grateful and repay back with her free services to the household.

"Nobody wants you, Charlotte, because you were born on the wrong side of life," were words that had been told to her over and over again by her mother's sister, because even her own maternal grandparents had refused to acknowledge her very existence. Charlie had never seen her mother's parents because they'd made it clear from the onset that she wasn't welcome into their lives or world. "A mistake like you shouldn't have come into this world at all because all you do is add more trouble to people."

Then Charlie forced the bad thoughts out of her mind and did as the pastor of the church she'd attended in Boston had once said.

"You are precious in the sight of the Lord and Jesus Christ gave His life for you. So never look down on yourself, nor allow anyone to make you feel that you're in this world by mistake. Our God never makes mistakes, and you were created with a purpose and have a bright destiny ahead of you. Whenever someone says heartbreaking words to you, replace them with the words of our Lord who said through the Prophet Isaiah in his forty-third chapter, that you are precious in His sight and

are honorable; therefore, you are loved. God will give men for you and people for your life. Never forget that! If there's one thing you must never forget, it's that you are precious in the sight of the Lord God."

Though the pastor had been preaching to the whole congregation, Charlie had held onto his words as a lifeline. Thereafter, whenever Aunt Lena or her four sons, Luke, Peter, John, and Simon spoke derogatory words to her, she would remind herself of that precious word given to her.

"I'm precious in the sight of the Lord," she murmured as she scrubbed the large washroom in the master bedroom, which was occupied by the head of the family, Mr. Harvey Chester. "I'm fearfully and wonderfully made, and the Lord's plans for my future will stand!"

A NEW HOME

"Charlotte, you need to smarten up and work fast like one who has life in them, not a corpse! How many times do I tell you how to do things one way and yet you go and do the exact opposite of my instructions? When will you ever learn?" Charlie was arranging cups and saucers onto a tray, and she tried not to get upset at Jacinta Grover's words. Mrs. Grover was the cook, and her tone was always so condescending whenever she spoke to Charlie. "Mr. Harvey and his brothers like everything to be in their proper place," she said. "You must make an effort to do as the masters require of us," then she shook her head and made a clicking sound with her tongue. "If Mrs. Chester were still alive, you wouldn't have lasted a single moment in this house. You're too slow!"

"I'm doing my best," Charlie said, holding herself back from hissing at the woman. It seemed as if nothing she ever did was good enough for this woman. She was the housekeeper, for crying out loud, not the cook or scullery maid. Yet Mrs. Grover treated her as if it was her work to serve and clean up. Charlie knew for a fact that Mr. Harvey had offered to have another maid brought in to help in the kitchen because of the amount of work to be done, but Mrs. Grover had said that she was able to manage things all on her own. Yet her way of managing was making Charlie take on tasks that weren't hers.

When Charlie had started working as the housekeeper in this house, Mrs. Lauren, Walter Chester's wife, had told her that her daily duties were to clean the whole house, do the laundry and make up the beds in all ten bedrooms. It wasn't much work according to Mrs. Grover, and so she was forced to take on kitchen duties.

Charlie didn't mind the hard work because she was used to it. She just minded the tone the woman used on her every single time, as if she were an imbecile who couldn't understand how to do the simplest house tasks.

"You're lucky to have been offered this position even without an interview, and it still puzzles me why," the older woman looked thoughtful. "But this is what happens when things are done without first consulting those who matter. I would have immediately told Mr. Harvey that he was making a mistake by offering such an important position to a person he'd never met before. There are plenty of other women I know of who would have made better housekeepers than yourself."

Charlie's response was to pick the tray up and leave the kitchen before she opened her mouth and said something unkind to the cook. The woman behaved in such a patronizing way, and it was beginning to irritate Charlie. Yet she didn't want any trouble because this would trickle to Sophie. Her cousin was just newly married to one of the five Chester brothers and Charlie didn't want her caught up in matters of the household staff. She would have to find a way to live with Mrs. Grover's continuous criticisms.

Once she was done setting the table for breakfast, she turned around and immediately walked into what seemed to be a wall.

"I'm sorry," Jesse Chester righted Charlie by placing both hands on her shoulders. "You seem to be in a hurry this morning."

"Yes, Sir," Charlie replied breathlessly. "I have to help Mrs. Grover so that breakfast isn't delayed." Then she still had her own household tasks to take care of.

From the moment she'd first set her eyes on this man, about six weeks ago when she and Sophie first arrived, it seemed as if her heart had been in a race that wasn't ending any time soon. No man had ever affected her in this way before, and it frightened her. She was twenty-eight years old, for crying out loud, not some young eighteen-year-old girl with stars in her eyes.

"Miss Charlotte?" Jesse bent down slightly and looked into her face. He was almost a head taller than she was, and she found his gray eyes to be quite mesmerizing. A woman could get lost in the beautiful eyes, she thought.

Jesse was concerned when the woman whose shoulders he held seemed dazed. He wondered if he'd hurt her when he'd bumped into her. His younger brothers George and Walter were always telling him that he was built like a huge boulder.

"Are you hurt?" He asked. "Miss Charlotte, are you all right?"

"Yes, Sir," Charlie blinked rapidly. "Please excuse me," she said, and quickly releasing herself from his hold, fled to the kitchen.

"Took your time now, didn't you?" Mrs. Grover said. Charlie clenched her fists and took a deep breath. "So incompetent," the older woman muttered.

Charlie, she told herself. *Just know that she's hurting so she wants to hurt someone else.*

From the little snitches of conversation she'd overheard from some of the cowboys when she'd once gone to the barn to get milk, Mrs. Grover's husband had left her for a younger woman. She didn't have any children and the man had put the younger woman in the family way, then they eloped. That was three years ago, and Mrs. Grover apparently hadn't recovered from that humiliation. *Poor woman, Charlie, just learn to be patient with her.*

"Did you say something?" Mrs. Grover gave her a sharp look.

"No, Ma'am," Charlie poured the oatmeal into an open jug and placed it on the tray. She also took the scrambled eggs Mrs. Grover had prepared and placed them in a covered dish. The older woman had already cut thick slices of bread and buttered them. She added a bowl of fruit and made Charlie carry everything to the dining room. Once Charlie had placed the tray on the table, she went to wake the children up. Alison and Alicia were Sophie's nieces by marriage, and Charlie loved the little girls. They'd come to Moonbeam Ranch with Glenda, who was married to one of Sophie's younger brothers-in-law, the one named Joseph.

"Aunt Charlie," Alison raised her arms in the air. "Please carry me," the three-year-old stuttered.

"No, carry me," Alicia started jumping up and down on the bed.

"Girls, please calm down," Charlie was laughing. The twins were adorable, and even though Mrs. Grover always grumbled about them, Charlie chose to ignore her. Alicia and Alison were just children and actually very well behaved. Everyone in the household loved them, except the often-sullen cook. After knowing that Mrs. Grover couldn't have children of her own, Charlie often thought that she should be kinder to other people's offspring.

The twins were always very careful to stay out of Mrs. Grover's way. Even though they were only three years old, they could already tell friend from foe.

"Where's Rusty?" Alison looked around the room for their puppy. Charlie had a bad feeling when the puppy was nowhere to be found. He always slept in the twins' bedroom and was a well-behaved little puppy.

The scream, yelp and crash that came from the kitchen gave Charlie the answer she sought.

"Oh no!" Charlie thought. The puppy must have slipped out of the room as soon as she'd opened the door. How hadn't she seen the furry little rascal? She ran out of the room and to the kitchen.

There was chaos everywhere, with Mrs. Grover screeching at the top of her voice and the dog yapping excitedly as it licked the milk on the floor while evading blows from the middle-aged woman. She had a long broom in her hands and was swatting at the little puppy. Luckily for Rusty, he kept dodging the blows.

"Stop!" Charlie cried out. "You'll hurt the puppy," she knelt and scooped the animal up in one hand.

Unfortunately, Mrs. Grover had let loose a hard blow with the broom and it descended toward Charlie's back just as Jesse walked into the kitchen.

Jesse moved very fast and jumped between the broom and Charlie's back, snatching it from Mrs. Grover's hand before the heavy blow landed.

"What do you think you're doing, Mrs. Grover?" He gave her a cold look. "When did it become all right for you to strike any of the other servants in the house?"

"Sir," the woman looked shaken and scared that one of her masters had found her in such a position. "It was the dog." Her face was very pale, and Charlie pitied her. "The puppy tripped me, and I dropped the pitcher of milk. I was trying to swat the dog away so I could clean up this mess."

"So, you tried to hit Miss Charlotte instead? Was she the one who tripped you? Was it her fault? Imagine if I hadn't gotten here sooner and snatched the broom from you, Miss Charlotte would have ended up with terrible bruises on her back."

"Sir," Charlie felt she had to speak up and defend Mrs. Grover. "Rusty was making a nuisance of himself, and Mrs. Grover was only trying to stop him from hurting himself and destroying things in the kitchen."

"I know what I saw," Jesse narrowed his eyes. "That doesn't excuse the fact that she tried to hit you with a broom. What if she'd succeeded and struck you, or what if it had been Alison or Alicia? Do you know what Joe would have done?"

"I'm sorry, Sir; it won't happen again," Mrs. Grover said.

"See that it doesn't happen again," Jesse dropped the broom, then held out his hands. "Give me that puppy." Charlie handed it over as she rose to her feet. "I'll keep it away from the kitchen. Let the twins know that I have the puppy."

"Yes, Sir," Charlie said. She expected Mrs. Grover to thank her for standing up for her before Jesse. Instead, the woman gave her a disdainful look and then turned her back on her.

Charlie sighed inwardly and went to prepare the twins for the day. For the rest of the day, she was careful not to do anything that would make Mrs. Grover even more vexed with her. Charlie knew that the woman was seething because Jesse had dared to defend her, a mere servant. But she hadn't asked for any help from him.

∼

"How long before dinner?" Jesse's voice startled Charlie and she nearly dropped the pan she was carrying to the large sink. Mrs. Grover had gone to her house to lock up her windows and had told Charlie not to serve dinner before her return. "I can see that it's ready so why the delay?"

Jesse walked over to the large stove and took off the lid from one of the pots. He wrinkled his nose, "I told Mrs. Grover not to use garlic," he said. "Alicia and Alison don't like it."

Charlie stared helplessly as he opened up all the four pots and made comments about the food. The cabbage was too watery and overcooked, the mashed potatoes looked dry, and the pot roast had too much garlic in it. Even the soup wasn't appealing to him.

"Serve dinner right now, we might as well eat before it gets cold and unappetizing," he said, just as Mrs. Grover walked back into the kitchen. From her narrowed eyes, Charlie knew that she'd overheard Jesse's last remark. But she said nothing as she ordered Charlie to prepare the serving bowls.

Once dinner was over, Charlie went to clear the table, but Lauren, Glenda and Sophie beat her to it. They carried the dirty plates and serving bowls into the kitchen.

"Thank you," Charlie said as she cleared the scraps of food from the plates. It troubled her that there was so much food left on each plate, and she wondered why her masters and mistresses didn't eat much. The only thing that was finished was the fruit cake that she'd baked just that afternoon and served as dessert. The large milk jug was empty too.

She was washing the dishes when she became aware that Mrs. Grover was watching her. She ignored the older woman because she had a feeling that she was spoiling for a fight.

"What did you tell Mr. Jesse?" Mrs. Grover asked.

"I don't understand," Charlie paused from washing the dishes and stared at the cook in puzzlement. "I haven't spoken to Mr. Jesse at all."

"Liar! I walked in and found you badmouthing my food to Mr. Jesse. What did you tell him?"

Charlie was about to open her mouth and defend herself when Jesse walked in. "Mrs. Grover, it's about to rain and I think you should leave for your house. I'll escort you to the gate and then ask one of the other men to see you safely to your house."

Charlie saw Mrs. Grover's lips tighten, but since the order had come from one of the masters, there was nothing she could do. Her eyes told Charlie that this was far from over, and the latter sighed inwardly.

DISMAL THOUGHTS

*J*esse Chester stretched out his long legs and then quickly pulled them back. His feet were cold. Then his nostrils were assailed with the sweet aroma of coffee, and he opened his eyes. It seemed as if he'd just gone to bed; then he had to wake up. He also became aware that someone was in his room. He peered through half-open eyes. It was Charlie.

She stood by the door, which was slightly open, as if prepared for flight.

"Mr. Harvey asked me to bring your coffee and wake you up because he needs you," she said.

"Thank you," Jesse sat up and reached for the coffee mug on his bedside table. He took a sip and nearly groaned out loud. This was the best coffee he'd tasted in a long time.

"You make very good coffee, Charlie," he said, being confident that their cook couldn't have prepared such delicious coffee.

Mrs. Grover made it too strong, and none of them liked it that way. Thanks to Harvey's insistence, they never had to drink Mrs. Grover's coffee ever again, not while Charlie was around. The first time Charlie had brewed the coffee and Harvey tasted it, he'd loved it and said that it should always be prepared in that way.

"Sir, Mr. Harvey wants you to join him in the dining room as soon as you can."

"Very well then, tell Harvey that I'll be with him shortly."

"Yes, Sir," Charlie said as she left the room.

Jesse stretched his aching limbs and got out of bed. It wasn't often that he was brought coffee in bed, and the last time it had happened was when he was ill. Harvey clearly wanted them to have an early start of the day. They were supposed to prepare for the shearing of a quarter of the flock, which was almost two thousand sheep. It was work that would take them a week to accomplish, and Jesse had to make arrangements for the nearly twenty shearers they hired every three months. The bunkhouse was full, and one of the smaller barns that housed ewes and their newborn lambs had been cleaned up and turned to sleeping quarters for the hired men. There was much work to be done and the bunkhouse cooks had their work cut out for them. But Jesse was confident that everything would go smoothly even with the increased number of hired men.

With George, Joe, and Walter, his younger brothers having recently married, most of the ranch work now fell on his and Harvey's shoulders. As the older ones, they'd decided to allow their brothers to enjoy their new statuses as married men. Harvey had given his brothers a year of light work around the ranch as they settled down with their new brides.

Of course, the three still helped out, but their workloads were very light. Harvey had said that he was doing things just as it was in Biblical days when men would be given a whole year off any kind of hard work so they could make their new brides happy.

Jesse finished his coffee, then washed and dressed, then carried the empty cup through to the kitchen. "Thank you for the coffee, Charlie. Good morning, Mrs. Grover."

"Good morning, Sir," Mrs. Grover responded with a smile. She was doing all she could to get back into his good books, but he felt that she was trying too hard. "Breakfast for you and Mr. Harvey will soon be ready. Charlotte is just setting the table and preparing everything you need."

"Thank you."

He smiled at Charlie, then walked to the dining room.

Harvey was waiting for him and motioned for him to take a seat.

"You know that it's just the two of us for these family meetings for the time being," Harvey said. "I'm sorry that I got you out of bed so early. But we need to get a head start on the shearing, so we're done within the week. I'm looking at four hundred animals per day among the twenty shearers. This means that each man has twenty animals to take care of."

"That's about right, though we also have to consider those ewes that are about to drop their lambs."

"I'll have the men separate those from the rest of the flock and probably deal with them first. But if a ewe is too terrified, we'll have to bypass her and wait until the next season." The men went on to discuss various matters to do with the ranch as Charlie served their breakfast.

Once she was done, she returned to the kitchen to prepare breakfast for the rest of the family under the watchful eyes of Mrs. Grover.

It was supposed to be Charlie's day off, and she wanted to be done quickly so she could go to town and purchase some fabric from the drapery store. She'd promised Glenda that she would make some frocks for the twins, and it was long overdue.

As she walked to town, Charlie thought about her life and how she'd come to Moonbeam Ranch. She had to admit that she loved it here even if Mrs. Grover wasn't the easiest of persons to have around. Mercifully, the woman's hostility was slightly less after the incident the other day in the kitchen with Jesse and the puppy. "What a life," she thought as she absentmindedly waved to someone she'd seen in church. She remembered that he had recently wedded; that was after Sophie. There were also two other weddings coming up in the next few days, and Charlie wondered when her own turn would come. Would she ever find a man who would love her unconditionally? Did such a person exist? She saw love every single day in the Chester household. The three married men loved and cherished their wives, and sometimes Charlie felt envious of them. Then she would remind herself that envy was a vice and shouldn't be found among those who profess to love the Lord.

"When will it be my turn, Lord," she murmured as she approached town. Another deep and abiding love had been what her own parents had shared. Her parents had loved each other very much, and even though they'd both been dead for over twenty years, the sweet memories of their happy home were always fresh in her mind. Though they didn't have much in the way of earthly possessions, their home had been filled with much love and laughter. Sadly, when she'd turned seven, her parents had died within days of each other and left her alone in the world, or so she'd thought at the time.

She'd gone to stay with the pastor of the church she and her parents had attended. Pastor Lionel and his wife were nice people and had opened their door to her even though they didn't have much. Charlie had thought that the family would adopt her, and they'd been ready to do so because everyone believed that she had no other living relatives. But then her mother's younger sister, Aunt Lena Morrison had come to visit. That was when seven-year-old Charlie had discovered that she had very wealthy relatives and that her mother's family was like royalty in Boston. Yet her mother had chosen the simple life because she'd fallen in love. The only crime Norah Parson had committed was to fall in love with one of the stable men who worked for the family.

As the eldest child and daughter, Norah had been expected to marry well. Her parents had even chosen a man for her, but she rejected him. Charlie chuckled softly to herself. Sophie was so much like Charlie's mother, who had fought for her love. No wonder she and Charlie loved each other and were very close.

Norah had been disowned by her parents, and when Charlie had lost her Pa and Ma, her grandparents had refused to even acknowledge her existence. It was only the shame of having one of their own being adopted by strangers and living in poverty that had made Aunt Lena take Charlie into her home.

That's when Charlie also found out how much her aunt had despised her mother for following her heart and love, not wealth. Charlie was treated worse than a maid in her own aunt's house, and the only person who'd showed her love and compassion right from the start was Sophie. It was because of Sophie that Charlie had learned how to read and write. It was also Sophie's old clothes, passed down to her that she'd worn, else she would have been naked.

Aunt Lena saw no need of allowing Charlie to go to school because she'd purposed that her sister's only child would work as a maid until she died of old age or otherwise.

Charlie had decided to run away from her aunt's house when she found an advertisement for a housekeeper all the way in Beaverhead, Montana. She still couldn't understand how, out of all the applications they'd received, Mr. Harvey and his brothers had chosen her own. And without an interview, they'd given her the position.

As she was getting ready to escape from her prison of nearly twenty-one years, Charlie had discovered the terrible plot against her cousin Sophie by her own brothers, mother, and the man who wanted to marry her by force. Sophie's four older brothers had drugged her food, with the plan being wholly approved of by their mother, but their father hadn't known about it. Then they carried Sophie to Mark Lander's house. The plan was to have her virtue compromised so she would be forced to marry the man.

Charlie had rescued her cousin, and together they'd made their way to Beaverhead and Moonbeam Ranch. Sophie had found the love of her life in George Chester, Jesse's brother.

Jesse Chester! Charlie sighed as she thought about the man who was giving her sleepless nights. How could she be falling in love with a man who was way out of her reach?

When Charlie had gone to live with Sophie and her family, she'd thought that her aunt and uncle were very wealthy. That's how it had been all her life, but just until she came to Moonbeam Ranch and saw what real wealth was. Yet the Chester family, all five gentlemen and their wives were such humble and down-to-earth people that it was difficult to tell that they were extremely wealthy. Sophie had whispered to Charlie that the Chester family was the wealthiest in Montana, but no one could tell from the way they conducted themselves.

The ranch had over fifty workers, and all of them were treated with kindness and respect. Not once had Charlie heard of any worker being treated unfairly. The married men had good homes built for them around the ranch, while the single ones lived in the bunkhouse that was well partitioned, so each man had his privacy.

When Aunt Lena and Uncle Brian Morrison, Sophie's parents and her four brothers Luke, Peter, John and Simon had come here about four weeks ago, Charlie had seen how impressed they'd been by the affluence they'd found. No wonder that they'd quickly allowed Sophie to get married to George, even though they'd brought Mark Lander along, probably hoping to convince Sophie to marry him. In the end, Mark had lost out, and George Chester had won Sophie's hand.

Charlie was very happy for her cousin who'd found true love with George. Sophie deserved the best things in life because she was such a kind-hearted and compassionate person. Not once in all her life, had Sophie treated Charlie as if she were beneath her, and that had often irked her Aunt Lena.

It didn't take Charlie long to get all she needed from the store, and she set out to return home. She'd also remembered to buy some boiled sugar candy for Alison and Alicia, or else the twins would never let her be.

"Someone looks happy," Jesse's voice startled her from her thoughts.

"Where did you come from?" She asked in surprise. "I thought you would be out on the range with all the shearing that's going on."

Jesse grinned at her, "Charlie, there's a reason we hire extra hands to help," he looked at her basket. "That looks heavy," and before she could even protest, he took the basket from her.

"What are you doing?" Charlie felt very self-conscious. People were staring at them, and she felt like they were wondering why one of the Chester men would be walking around with a servant.

"It's not too heavy," Charlie tried to protest, but Jesse kept the basket away from her.

"I was done supervising the shearers and decided to stretch my legs a bit. It was Glenda who told me that you'd come to town, and I hurried after you."

Charlie looked around for Jesse's horse, a big, black stallion that suited him very well, but he was nowhere to be found.

"I left the horse at home because I wanted to spend time walking with you," Jesse said when he rightly guessed that she was looking about for his horse.

"Mr. Chester..."

"Charlie, my name is Jesse and I want you to get used to using it. Mr. Chester was our father, as Harvey will tell you."

"People are really staring at us," Charlie said in a low voice.

Jesse looked around and indeed met the curious looks of various people. He waved at them, and some responded and turned to mind their business while others just continued staring. "I want to give them something to stare at," he said, and with his free hand, took Charlie's and held it. "Now let them not only stare but talk. This is what life in a small town looks like," he grinned at her. "When people are idle, they need something to do, so let's give them the task of running around to tell whoever will care to listen that Jesse Chester has found himself a beautiful young woman and they've been seen holding hands around town."

"Jesse!" Charlie's face was red as a beetroot, and her shyness really appealed to Jesse.

He hadn't stopped thinking about this woman from the first day he'd seen her, nearly two months ago when she and his sister-in-law, Sophie, first arrived at Moonbeam Ranch.

Her gentle smile, soft blue eyes and calmness warmed his heart. For one who'd been disappointed by love twice, Jesse had held his heart from going after another, but he began to suspect that Charlie had found her way into his affections.

"You work too hard, Charlie," he commented as they drew closer to home. Charlie noticed that a man seemed to be following them.

"Who is that man?" She looked over her shoulder. She was afraid but glad that Jesse was with her. She hadn't noticed him on her way to town. "Jesse, I'm scared."

Jesse barely spared the man a glance. "Don't mind too much about him. He's there to protect us. And besides, why should you be scared when the Lord has His eyes on you all the time, and when I'm here with you?"

"What?"

Jesse smiled at her, "Charlie, there are many enemies abroad and we always have to be very careful. Please promise me that you'll never go out alone again. It's just too risky."

Charlie laughed shortly, "I'm just a nobody, what would anyone want with me?"

"Don't ever say that again, Charlie. You're a member of our family by marriage and so a target of some twisted mind too. I want you to be safe always."

Charlie shivered slightly, "Then I'll never leave the house again."

Jesse threw his head back and laughed out loud. "Charlie, I didn't mean to frighten you into becoming a self-declared prisoner at home. As long as you're careful and inform one of us that you want to go out, we'll provide an escort for you. The person will be very unobtrusive and won't attract attention, so you won't even know that he's there, but he'll keep you safe."

"Thank you," Charlie said as they approached the front door. "You've been good company for me."

"Likewise," Jesse said. Before they parted ways at the front door, he placed her basket on the floor then touched her cheek lightly. "You're a very beautiful woman," he said, and before Charlie could formulate any response, he was gone.

∼

"What was all that about?" Sophie walked into Charlie's room later that evening after dinner.

Charlie looked at her in puzzlement. She was folding the twins' clothes and intended to take them to the nursery before going to bed. "What are you talking about, Sophie?'

"I saw you and Jesse walking down the driveway as if you'd come from a picnic. Where did you go?"

Charlie grinned at her cousin, "Someone is rather curious, I'll say."

"Charlie," Sophie sat on her bed and helped her to fold the clothes. "George and I were talking, and he said that he hasn't seen Jesse this happy in a long while. You make my brother-in-law very happy and I'm praying that something will come out of all this."

"No," Charlie gasped. "Sophie, don't talk like that. Jesse is way beyond me, and he only met me in town, and we walked back together. I went there to get fabric so I can make some dresses for Alicia and Alison."

"Charlie, please allow yourself to love and be loved. If Jesse asks for your hand, I'm your closest relative and believe me, I'll say a very loud yes."

"Sophie, don't get ahead of yourself. Mr. Jesse is just being kind to a servant in his household. Don't read more into all this. I doubt that he thinks of me in that way."

Sophie shook her head, "Charlie, you're such a lovely person and deserve to love and be loved. Please don't shut your heart toward Jesse."

Charlie thought about Sophie's words when she was lying in her bed and told herself that her cousin was only imagining things. Jesse Chester was wealthy beyond what Charlie could imagine. There were many women in Beaverhead who would do anything to become his wife. She'd seen women in church fluttering around Jesse and Harvey like little butterflies that were looking for a place to settle. Some even dared to come to the house and blatantly make it known that they were after the two remaining brothers.

What Charlie knew about some of the young women was that they came from wealthy families around Beaverhead, and Jesse would probably look that way when it was time for him to settle down and get married.

"Charlie, you're not some man's plaything," Sophie had told her about five years ago when one of her brother's friends had pretended to show an interest in Charlie. *"Don't allow any of my brother's friends to take advantage of you. You deserve a good man who will love and care for you and marry you in the right way. Be very careful and never allow flattery and lies to turn your head."*

Luke's friend had tried to buy Charlie gifts to convince her to bend to his will and whims, but she would give them to Sophie, who handed them back to the owner. It was a relief when she heard that the man was engaged and later got married to someone in his own circles.

From then on, Charlie told herself that every wealthy man was only out to take advantage of her, and she would never give them the chance to dishonor her. What if that was Jesse's intention? She was honest enough to admit to herself that holding hands with him had felt good. When she was little, she would see her parents holding hands all the time and her mother had told her that it brought them closer.

But Jesse was in another class altogether and Charlie could never hope to attain to his status. She didn't want him to toy with her emotions and then one day go ahead and marry someone else of his own class.

"Sophie was just jesting," she told herself as she allowed sleep to take over.

THE PURSUIT OF HAPPINESS

A few days later, Charlie was forced to stay up late because Mrs. Grover had retired early to her cottage on the other side of the homestead. The food that the cook had prepared for dinner lay uneaten and congealed with lard in the pots since no one was around for dinner.

Sophie, Glenda, and Lauren had taken the twins to visit Glenda's grandaunt who lived in one of the new cottages on the other side of the homestead. Jesse and his three brothers aside from George, were out there in the barn.

One of their prize mares was foaling, and she seemed to be having great difficulty because this was her first birth. George, who was still recuperating from a terrible accident a few weeks ago, was sleeping. Sophie had instructed Charlie that he wasn't to be disturbed in any way and would come to the kitchen for dinner whenever he was ready.

Charlie looked once more at the food in the large pot and grimaced. Mrs. Grover had made pork and mutton stew and it looked very unappetizing. She'd used too much garlic as usual and more lard than was necessary. Charlie had noticed that Mrs. Grover didn't seem to care what she prepared or served as long as it made it to the table. What the woman didn't realize, or if she did, she chose to ignore it, was that more and more food was being returned uneaten to the kitchen. Since Mrs. Grover didn't like baking or maybe she didn't know how, she always left that part to Charlie. All the desserts that Charlie served never returned to the kitchen. It was clear that the family preferred eating the dessert more than the main food.

Charlie knew that the family was no longer enjoying the elderly cook's food, but they were also too polite to tell her so. Yet so much food was going to waste and the only ones who enjoyed it were the guard dogs who enjoyed a feast every evening. Charlie would take the leftovers to the ten dogs after Mrs. Grover had left for her house.

Concerning the food in the pot, Mrs. Grover had left Charlie with instructions to reheat it and serve the men when they were done with the mare. By that time, the cook had said, the three women and the twins would also be back, so they could all eat their dinner together.

Charlie knew that no one would touch this food, not with the way it looked right now.

"I can't possibly serve this mess to the family," Charlie murmured just as the backdoor opened and Jesse walked into the kitchen. He looked tired and strained, and her heart went out to him.

"Are you all right?" She quickly asked him.

"No," Jesse sighed deeply. "Aurora Sunset isn't doing too well. The foal is a big one and as her first child it could be very risky for both mare and foal. The foal is refusing to bring out its head, and both mother and baby are in danger of sudden death. I came to find out if Sophie is back. We could use a doctor's help."

Charlie shook her head, "Mrs. Sophie isn't back yet. Have you prayed for Aurora Sunset?"

"What?"

"I mean, have you tried laying hands on the mare and praying for her?"

"What?" Jesse repeated as if he hadn't heard her very well. He gave her a perplexed look. "How do you mean?"

Charlie smiled, "Would you please take me to the horse?"

Jesse observed Charlie for a moment and realized that she was serious. He nodded.

"Follow me then."

The men in the stable, about ten of them, were standing in small groups, and the mare whined in pain as she walked around the part of the stable that had been prepared for the birthing process. Charlie ignored the questioning looks directed toward her as she walked up to the horse and reached out a tender hand. She touched Aurora Sunset's neck and began to rub in gentle small circles while speaking softly to the animal.

"What's going on?" Harvey started but was silenced by Jesse's raised hand.

Charlie's voice was soft and soothing, and within minutes Jesse noticed that the mare was calming down. But Charlie ignored the men as she spoke to the mare.

"Sweet mother, you only have a little way to go; then you'll see your beautiful little one," she crooned while rubbing the horse's neck. "I'll pray for you now," she said then took a deep breath.

"Our dear heavenly Father, our lives and indeed the lives of all creatures are in Your mighty and able hands. In the name of Your beloved Son Jesus Christ, I bring Aurora Sunset before You this evening. According to the time set for her, this is when she's ready to bring forth her offspring, for You gave the command for all Your creatures to be fruitful and multiply. Father, if every sparrow in this world is known by You and Your eyes are on them, then I know that You have Your loving eyes on Aurora Sunset and her foal. In the name of Jesus, through whom all things exist, please let this little one be released into this life and let mother and child be safe, amen."

"Harvey look," Walter cried out in astonished excitement as soon as Charlie said 'amen.' "The foal's head is out now."

"Charlie, you're truly God sent," Joe told her. "We've been hoping the head would move so we can assist her in bringing her child out. This is truly a miracle, thank you, Charlie."

"You're welcome," Charlie felt shy at the sudden respect she saw in the eyes of all the men present.

In no time the foal was born, and when Charlie realized that everyone's attention was away from her, she slipped out of the stable and returned to the house.

"Thank You, Lord," she was smiling broadly as she raised her hands heavenward. "Thank You for honoring your handmaid's prayer. Thank You for Aurora Sunset and her little one. Thank You for all the men who've worked so hard to make sure that the horse and foal are well. Bless them all, Lord," she said. "And especially Jesse," she added as an afterthought and then blushed at her prayer.

Jesse immediately noticed Charlie's absence as soon as she was gone, and he wanted to follow her. But there was still work to be done for the mare and her little one. As he assisted in getting the mare as comfortable as possible with her newborn, his thoughts were fixated on Charlie.

37

She was his sister-in-law by marriage through Sophie. The two women were very close, yet Charlie never took advantage of that relationship to slacken at her work. If anything, she worked even harder.

Charlie had come to Moonbeam Ranch as a housekeeper, and she was very diligent at her work. The woman asked for nothing more than her weekly wages, yet she could have anything else she wanted or needed because her cousin was married to a Chester!

"Jesse, get your mind back to work," Harvey's sharp reprimand made him blink. He noticed that the mare and her foal had been taken into one of the stalls where it was warm and were resting on a clean bed of straw. One of the workers had even finished cleaning up the mess.

Jesse did what he could to finish up, then followed Harvey out of the stable. "Jess, are you all right?" His older brother asked in concern. "Lately I notice that you've been rather absentminded. Is there anything going on in your life that I should know about?"

Jesse sighed, looking around to make sure that it was just the two of them. "Harvey, how does one tell when love is real or not?"

"Why do you ask such a strange question?"

"Because you know that I've been let down twice by women I thought I was in love with, yet it turned out to be nothing but infatuation," he shook his head.

"Remember how Miss Sandra Court turned out to be nothing but a money-seeking and status-hungry woman, while Miss Martha Lewis was no better. Remember how I brought Miss Lewis all the way from New Jersey, only for me to find out that she wasn't right for me. How will I ever know the right woman for me, Harvey? See how our three brothers have found true love with such wonderful women. Lauren, Glenda, and Sophie are answers to prayers that our brothers made. That's the kind of love that my heart yearns for, yet I don't want to open up and get broken down again."

"Oh, Jess!" Harvey placed a light hand on his brother's shoulder. "Love can be very simple and complex at the same time. I'll say that you should pray about it and trust that the Lord will send the right woman for you. God's time is always the best."

"I've been praying, Harvey, but I'm still confused. I don't ever want to make a mistake and end up being married to the wrong woman. For me, marriage is forever, and I can't imagine living in misery for the rest of my life because of making a mistake in choice."

"I wish I could tell you that finding the right person is easy. I think your heart will just know when this person comes along. For one, you'll experience so much peace with them around you. Jess, when you find the woman your heart yearns for, hold onto her very tight and never let go," Harvey's voice dropped to a soft whisper and his expression became strange. "When you find the right woman for you, never listen to anyone who tries to come in between you and her. For if you find her and then through carelessness you let her go, just know that you'll regret that for the rest of your life." And having said that, Harvey dropped his hand, gave Jess a pitiful look and walked away.

Jess stared at his brother's retreating back in astonishment.

"What just happened?" He asked himself. "Did I say something wrong to Harvey?"

Then he shrugged and thought back to the past. He knew that his brother had been deeply wounded, but Harvey was never one to share his private feelings and thoughts with anyone. Jesse was very sure that all of Harvey's pain was because of Salome Franklin, the young woman who'd lived with them for a few weeks. Everyone had thought she was a servant and so had Jesse, but he'd seen the way Harvey looked and acted around her. Then suddenly Sally had left, and he was the one who'd driven her to their pastor's house when his mother ran her out of the home. Jesse had never told Harvey or any of his other brothers that he'd overheard their mother threatening Sally. The words she'd spoken to Sally weren't clear, but her tone had said it all. That's when Jesse had suspected that Sally was more than just a servant and she meant so much to Harvey. After she was gone, Harvey had never been the same again. Yes, he smiled and went about life as usual, but Jesse could see the brokenness in him since then.

"Poor Harvey," Jesse thought, even as he wondered where Sally was. Seven years had gone by, and he'd never heard his brother talk about Sally. This was actually the first time they'd ever shared anything about love.

Harvey had said that the heart would recognize the woman.

"I think I already have her," Jesse said as he made his way to the house.

KNOWING HER PLACE

A Few Days Later

"I'm sorry," Charlie stammered and stared guiltily at Jesse. He'd walked out of the kitchen, and she'd thought he was done with breakfast and gone for the morning, only for him to return abruptly and catch her eating food from his plate. "It's just that I hate to waste anything," she still held the dry slice of bread in her hand, one she'd picked up from the plate he'd pushed aside. That morning Jesse had decided to have his breakfast in the kitchen because he'd overslept and been late to join the rest of the family. Mrs. Grover had served him bread, scrambled eggs, and some ham. He'd eaten almost everything and left a slice of bread. That's what Charlie was holding in her hand.

Jesse stared in shock at what was on Charlie's plate. It didn't look like fresh food but scraps from other dishes and plates. It seemed as if she'd collected whatever had remained from the other breakfast plates to make a meal for herself. What was going on here?

"Why are you eating that, Charlie?" He pointed at her plate. "That's what's meant to be fed to the dogs," he walked into the pantry to check and see if they were out of food. The pantry was full as usual, and he stood there wondering whatever was going on. The egg basket was full, and he could even see a joint of cured ham sitting on one of the shelves. There was also plenty of freshly baked bread. Yet Charlie was eating leftovers!

Before Charlie could respond to Jesse's question, Mrs. Grover walked into the kitchen from outside. She didn't immediately notice Jesse who was standing at the pantry door.

"You're lucky that I even let you eat those scraps," Mrs. Grover said. "You need to go hungry so that you'll know your place in this house. Who told you to prepare more food last night when I'd already done so? People like you are very wasteful and think that you can do as you like. I'm the cook in this house, and you're nothing but the cleaner so you have no business interfering with my work. Well, I'll show you that you're nothing but a lowly servant even if you feel that your cousin is a member of the family."

"Is that right?" Jesse couldn't believe that their cook was

responsible for Charlie eating the crumbs from their table. Even their dogs and the barn cats ate better!

"Oh, Mr. Jesse!" Mrs. Grover paled when she saw him. "I didn't see you standing there."

"Clearly!" He said in a very cold voice. He looked furious, and Charlie felt a little scared of him at this moment. "How long has this been going on? When was the last time Charlie had a proper meal in this house?"

"Sir, it's really nothing," Charlie had never seen Jesse looking this furious. "This food is all right for me."

"And I say that it's not," he hissed through clenched teeth. "Mrs. Grover, what did you mean by saying that Charlie needs to know her place in this household?"

"Sir," the woman looked very nervous. "I didn't mean anything by it. I was only jesting."

"Yet I heard you saying those words out loud. I ask again, how long has Charlie been eating the scraps from our table when there's plenty of food and we've never denied anyone anything from this kitchen? I had to enter the pantry to see if we're out of food and saw that all the tins and bins are full. Why is Charlie eating food that is fit for dogs and cats?"

Mrs. Grover was at a loss for words, and for a moment, Charlie felt sorry for her. She wanted to tell Jesse that the scraps she'd been feeding on in this house were so much better than what she'd been forced to eat in Aunt Lena's house back in Boston.

"Mrs. Grover, you've been with this family for many years, and I thought that by now you would have known the kind of people we are. How dare you treat a member of this household as badly as this?" Jesse picked up the plate that was in front of Charlie and emptied its contents into Rusty's dish. "This is totally unacceptable, and Harvey must hear about this. What nonsense and audacity do you have to do this?"

"Please, Sir," Mrs. Grover pleaded. "It was a mistake on my part, and I won't ever repeat it again."

"I have a feeling that a lot has been happening in this house, and we've not been aware of it. Well now it all ends here. I don't want you in this kitchen again until I've spoken with Harvey about this matter."

"Sir?" Mrs. Grover stared disbelievingly at Jesse.

"You heard me, Mrs. Grover. I was very clear and you're not deaf. Now, please go home and wait to hear from us." And Jesse stood in the kitchen until the older woman had left.

Then he turned to Charlie, "Miss Charlotte, now tell me everything that's been happening to you under Mrs. Grover's hand and why you chose to remain silent in your suffering? Why keep something so terrible like this hidden from us?"

"Sir, you're taking it all the wrong way." Charlie didn't want to add any more trouble to what Mrs. Grover was already dealing with. This whole thing had started a few days ago. Mrs. Grover would make her serve all the breakfast food and carry it to the dining room without leaving anything for her in the pot. It was actually the only meal that the family ate without leaving much on their plates. Charlie was then forced to eat whatever was left over from the main table, and when she'd dared to ask Mrs. Grover about this, she'd been harshly rebuked.

"Who do you think you are to ask me such a question? Whenever I prepare food, it's for my masters and the whole family, and not some servant. Charlotte, you've been presuming too much, and I wonder what gave you such audacity to question me about the food I serve. You're nothing but a maid in this house and you need to know your place."

Charlie hadn't said a word further and decided to hold her peace. In any case, whatever was often left over was sufficient for her needs. But the same thing had happened during all the other mealtimes. Charlie didn't mind missing food during the other mealtimes because whatever Mrs. Grover prepared was terrible and barely edible.

Then last evening Charlie had thought that Mrs. Grover was gone for the night, and she was so hungry and desperate, she'd boiled two eggs and cut herself two slices of bread. Mrs. Grover had come in and found her just about to eat and had carried the food and poured it all into the dustbin. Charlie had gone to bed hungry, and sleep had been a long time coming.

"Miss Charlotte," Jesse's voice reminded her that he was still present. "I'm waiting for an explanation of all that's been happening to you."

"Sir, it's really nothing," Charlie said weakly, hoping he would drop the whole issue.

Jesse realized that Charlie wasn't going to say anything. This all reminded him of when his sister-in-law, Lauren had first come to Moonbeam Ranch. She'd been ill-treated by their then housekeeper, Mrs. Rowan, and Harvey hadn't taken it lightly. Indeed, none of them had.

"I'll let this go for now because I know that even if we stay here for a whole day and night, you won't say a word. But when I tell Harvey about this, there'll be some explaining to do."

"Must you tell him? Please just let it go," Charlie pleaded.

"That's not for you to say," he told her. "Such behavior is unacceptable to all of us, and we won't have it."

"What if you kept it between the three of us? Mrs. Grover won't do it again."

"You're right, Mrs. Grover won't ever treat a member of this household so abominably again because she no longer works here."

"But, Sir..." Charlie spluttered.

Jesse held up his hand, "I've said my piece, and there's no going back. This is my decision and I know my brothers and their wives will back me up on it. Every person in this house is important and should be treated with kindness and respect. Mrs. Grover has disrespected you on two occasions that I personally have witnessed. I'm very sure that she'd done more in my absence."

"Temper your justice with mercy, Sir. Please."

"Even the Bible in Matthew Chapter five, verse seven says, *Blessed are the merciful, for they will receive mercy*," he said.

"And that's all that I'm going to say about this matter, Miss Charlotte. Just know that Mrs. Grover no longer works in this house."

"Jesse, please."

"Charlie," his look was stern, "I can do anything for you but not this one. Let it be," and before she could plead more, he was gone.

TRIALS AND TRIBULATIONS

Charlie woke up very early the next morning. Mrs. Grover was gone, and it now fell on her to prepare all the meals until a new cook was brought in.

Walking into the dimly lit kitchen, Charlie gave a little startled cry when she saw someone sitting at the table. Her heart returned to normal when she realized that it was Jesse, and he was peeling some potatoes.

"You're going to need a lot of help this morning because it's your first as our full-time cook, well, at least for the time being," he said. "And just so you know, your wages go up, commensurate with the work you're expected to do."

"But you didn't have to wake up early too. I can manage very well on my own, Sir," she protested as she walked into the pantry and took down an apron from behind the door. "Why are you up so early?" She brought out oatmeal flour from the pantry. "Are you done with the shearing?"

"I'm almost done, but this year the sheep have such thick wool that it's taking more time than we expected."

"Is that a good or bad thing?" Charlie placed a pot of water on the stove.

"It's a good thing because this means that there are more earnings from the thick wool. But it's rather uncomfortable for the poor sheep, carrying that heavy load around all the time. Believe me, you can almost see the relief in their tiny eyes when the wool is taken off their backs and bodies."

"The Lord gives every creature only the load that they're able to carry," Charlie said.

"Amen to that," Jesse said. "Charlie, I've been meaning to ask you, how is it that you don't come to church with us on Sundays?"

Charlie gave him a guilty smile. "But I've never missed a single Sunday service, just so you know."

"How's that? You've never travelled to church with us, at least I don't recall seeing you in any of the buggies."

"I walk," Charlie said simply, ignoring Jesse's intense stare. "And when I get to church, I like sitting at the back."

"We have a family pew, two in fact and all members of the household are free to sit there."

"Ah well," Charlie said, as she entered the pantry and returned with a basket of eggs.

When Charlie laid breakfast out, Jesse was quite impressed. He'd watched as she worked swiftly and efficiently making oatmeal porridge, boiling milk, and making her delicious coffee, and she fried the eggs too. She added freshly baked scones dripping with honey to the tray, which she carried into the dining room.

"How is it that we don't eat like this every single day?" Harvey asked as he bit into a flaky donut. "These are very delicious, and I think I'll have another one or maybe two more."

"Charlie baked them last night when we'd all gone to bed," Jesse said. "I woke up in the middle of the night to go and check on the mare that's about to drop its foal and found her busy baking these delicious scones. I didn't want to disturb or startle her, so I used the exit door in the study instead of coming into the kitchen."

"Charlie always does that whenever she's upset by something," Sophie said. "Did something happen to Charlie yesterday?"

Jesse noticed that she was glaring at him.

He quickly told them everything that had happened before, from the time Mrs. Grover had nearly struck Charlie with a broom and then about her eating the leftovers from their plates.

"I didn't believe it when Charlie even said that she usually walks to church. Why doesn't she sit at table for meals with us? How is it that we've not thought about Charlie's welfare in this house before?"

Jesse noticed that Sophie looked uncomfortable. "Sophie, you know Charlie better than all of us. Has she always been this reserved and private?"

"You've got to understand that since she was seven and came to live with my family, a lot of things changed for her," Sophie said.

"In what way?" Jesse wanted to know everything about the woman who occupied his thoughts these days. He was free to ask questions because he knew that Charlie was out of the house. Usually at this time, he'd realized, she was out in the chicken coop cleaning it and collecting eggs.

Sophie sighed, "You all saw my family when they came here a few weeks ago," everyone nodded. "Mama's sister, my Aunt Norah was Charlie's mother. As the eldest daughter of her family, Aunt Norah was expected to marry a man chosen for her by her family because of prestige and social standing. But she committed the worst sin according to the Parsons."

"The Parsons?" Jesse asked. "Who are they?"

"That's my Mama's family. They're steel magnates, and Aunt Norah didn't follow the norm of marrying money and status. She fell in love with one of the stable men, and that was her doom. The family disowned her, and my grandparents never wanted anything to do with her again. So, when Aunt Norah and her husband died, no one wanted to take Charlie, not even my grandparents. She was only seven years old at the time, a year older than me. The pastor of their church wanted to adopt Charlie, but fear of shame and ridicule by society forced my mother to take her sister's daughter in, but she was never once treated like she belonged to the family." Sophie looked down and Jesse saw the shame on her face. "Charlie was never once invited to eat with us at the table. She never went to school because she was treated worse than a servant."

"But why?" Jesse couldn't believe that someone could turn their back on someone who was their blood relative.

"According to what my grandparents said at the time, the shame of knowing that they have a stable man's child as a granddaughter was something they could never accept."

"That still doesn't explain why Charlie is so reserved," Harvey said.

"That's because my Mama and brothers told her that she can never belong to any family. They called her an outcast who wasn't wanted by anyone. If you recall, when my family was here, they wanted to take Charlie back to Boston with them, but I refused."

"You did the right thing," Jesse said.

"My mother believes that Charlie doesn't deserve to fall in love and get married because she'll only add more shame to the family."

"How can she say that?"

"Mama said that the only kind of man who would be interested in Charlie is probably a stable man like her father, or even worse."

Everyone looked shocked. "That's such a terrible thing for anyone to say to her niece."

"Yes, Jess, so Mama said she would never allow Charlie to get married and bring more shame to the family by descending even lower than her own mother. According to Mama, she'd rather that Charlie should remain as an old maid and be her servant all the days of her life. Charlie was never allowed to eat at the table with us. She had to go to church but couldn't ride in the family carriage and had to walk."

Jesse shut his eyes briefly and felt shame wash over him on behalf of families like his. And then Mrs. Grover had to go and continue making Charlie feel like she was a nobody! Well, good riddance to that awful woman and Jesse purposed to always look out for Charlie from then on.

∼

It was early dawn when Charlie heard the neighing of a horse. She frowned slightly because the sound was a foreign one. She told herself that she knew the sounds that all the horses around the homestead made. Each one had a peculiar sound, much like people's voices. As she listened, she heard the rumbling of wheels on the cobbled driveway. That was definitely a carriage and she wondered who the early morning visitor was.

As the housekeeper and cook, it fell to her to get the door, so she hurried out of bed. She didn't want the visitor using the loud knocker and waking the whole household up. So, she rushed to the door and flung it open just as a woman as young as Lauren was about to knock.

"It's about time too," the woman said haughtily and pushed past Charlie, rolling her long white gloves off. An older version of the first woman also breezed into the living room.

"You must be the maid," the younger woman said with a slight sneer on her lips. "Get our luggage in and take it to our rooms," she ordered.

Charlie stood there staring at the two women and wondering who they were. She couldn't recall anyone telling her that they would be having guests and from the look of things, they were here for a long stay.

"Don't just stand there like an imbecile," the older woman snapped. "Hop to it and make sure you don't steal anything while you're at it."

"Aunt Veronica, it's still too early in the morning to be ordering people around," Jesse's voice made Charlie sigh in relief because she'd been about to snap at the visitors.

"Oh Jesse," Aunt Veronica said, holding her arms wide open. "You seem to grow more handsome every time I see you. I think it's time that I found you a wife. Where are your brothers?" The woman demanded.

"Aunt Vero, it's not yet six and you're being too loud. We have children in the house and other people are still resting," he turned to the younger woman. "Cousin Sheila, you look as beautiful as always."

"Thank you," the woman laughed coyly while patting down her hair. "You don't look too bad yourself."

"No husband still?" Charlie hid her smile at Jesse's mocking tone. "I expected that by now you'd have snagged some poor fish and made him your husband. What's it been, three or four years since we last saw each other? You must admit that you're not getting any younger, dear cousin. Girls your age already have two or three children and even another on the way. What are you waiting for?" Jesse taunted his cousin. These were his least favorite relatives and even though they didn't have many relatives, he preferred that these folks keep their distance. Aunt Veronica and her daughter were well-known snobs even though they weren't wealthy.

Aunt Vero's husband was a railroad engineer, but she and her daughter behaved as if he were Cornelius Vanderbilt himself! In the past when his mother was alive and they'd visited, Aunt Vero would beg for money, and that hadn't stopped after her sister's death. Three years ago, had been their last visit until now. At the time, Aunt Vero had tried to get Harvey to give her their mother's jewelry because she felt that she was entitled to it.

Of course, her demands had vexed Harvey so much that they woke up one morning to find a carriage waiting to convey them to the train station and back home to San Francisco. She'd stopped writing to find out how they were doing, and Jesse had a feeling that this visit had something to do with wanting money. He just hoped Harvey wouldn't give into the woman's scheming ways.

"Or are all the men in San Francisco blind? I mean, they have the world's most beautiful woman living in their midst," Jesse's tone was full of mockery and his cousin pouted at him.

"Jesse, would you stop with that?" Harvey walked into the living room and gave him a sharp look, but Jesse merely shrugged. "Welcome to Moonbeam, Aunt Vero and Cousin Sheila." He looked at the luggage which one of the cowboys was just carrying into the house. "You seem to have come for a lengthy visit and didn't let us know. I hope Uncle Alfred is all right."

"I haven't seen my dear sister's sons in years," Aunt Veronica said, ignoring his question about her husband. "I heard that Joe, George, and Walter are now married. Why wasn't I invited to the weddings? I came to make sure that they married women who are worthy of them. I'm the nearest thing to a mother that you boys have, and it pains me that none of your brothers bothered to invite me to their weddings."

Jesse laughed, "Aunt Vero, my brothers are of age and can answer for themselves. Since you've decided that you're staying for a while, you'll have ample time to ask them whatever questions you want about their weddings and wives."

Jesse noticed his brother Harvey giving him an odd look. He ignored Harvey and turned to Charlie.

"Come with me, Miss Charlotte, there's something I need you to get for me from the kitchen."

Charlie was glad to leave the presence of the formidable women who looked like snobs. She smiled when she thought about how Jesse had put down the younger one, then she rebuked herself for gloating at another's misfortune. That was very unchristian like!

～

"Jesse, your attitude towards Aunt Vero and Sheila was totally uncalled for, especially in the presence of a servant," Harvey caught up with Jesse on his way to the stable.

"First of all, Charlie isn't merely a servant, and secondly, even you don't want those people here. Aunt Vero and Sheila are bothersome characters, and I don't even know what they're doing here."

"Be that as it may, it isn't kind or nice to speak to them in such tones. Charlie will think that we treat our poor relatives with disdain. Please see that it doesn't happen again."

Jesse hadn't thought of it in that way, and he felt ashamed of himself. "I'm sorry, I'll apologize to our relatives when I return from the range."

Harvey gave him a curt nod. "Or better still, keep out of their way. Any apology to Aunt Vero will only give her cause to make her unreasonable demands. Let me handle them from here on out. Tell the others to steer clear of them for the time being."

"Will do, big brother," Jesse saluted him and entered the stable to begin his day's chores.

When he went to the house for lunch, he didn't find his aunt and cousin. "They've gone to visit friends," Charlie told him as she served his lunch. "What you did this morning wasn't really nice, Jesse," she said in a quiet voice. "I observed your relatives to be obnoxious, but you don't have to descend to their level. Most arrogant and snobbish people only thrive when you give them your attention."

Jesse bowed his head, "I hear you, Charlie, and I promise that it won't happen again. But I didn't like the way they were talking to you."

"Jess, people will always talk down to those they feel are inferior to them. You won't always be around to defend me, so let me learn how to cope with them. Besides, you're lucky to have relatives who come to check up on you from time to time."

Jesse wanted to tell Charlie that he suspected his aunt to have come visiting because she wanted to beg for money. With Aunt Vero, it was never borrowing, because she would never return it. But then he remembered that it wasn't kind to talk about people behind their backs. That was gossip, which was a terrible vice.

"I hear you, Charlie. Where are my brothers?"

"Mr. Harvey already ate, while Mr. Joe and Mr. Walter are still out on the range. Mr. George is resting in his room."

Jesse chuckled softly, "Please stop referring to all of us as 'mister' because the title makes us all sound really old."

Charlie smiled, "I'm doing it because Mrs. Vero and Miss Sheila are around. I don't want them to think that the servant is disrespecting them. Which brings me to another issue, when are you bringing in another cook? I can't continue to handle the housekeeping and all the cooking at the same time."

"I think Harvey mentioned finding another housekeeper and not a cook. You're doing a wonderful job, Charlie. No one will want to taste another person's food after eating yours."

Charlie felt herself blushing at the open praise. "Thank you for saying that."

"Just giving credit where it's due."

∼

"Where is Charlie?" Jesse looked up when his brother asked the question. Harvey was standing at his place at the head of the table. Just that morning he'd ordered their resident carpenter to fashion a larger table and the twenty-seat piece of furniture had been delivered to the house in the early afternoon."

"Why are you asking about the maid?" Aunt Vero was seated at the foot of the table, the place reserved for the mistress of the household. Jesse wished he could tell her to move and sit elsewhere but he'd promised Harvey that he would stay out of trouble with their relatives.

"Charlie!" Harvey barked, ignoring his aunt. "Charlotte!"

"Yes, Sir," a flustered Charlie came running to the dining room, wiping her floury hands on the apron around her waist. She'd been preparing flour to bake bread when she heard the senior master calling her.

"We're waiting for you," Harvey said.

"Sir?" She stared at him in confusion then at the heavily laden table. To her knowledge, she'd brought everything that was needed for dinner to the table. "Did I leave anything out?"

Harvey gave her a gentle smile, "No, tonight I'd like us to all have dinner together as a family."

Aunt Vero hissed, but when Harvey gave her a long look, she bowed her head and remained silent.

"I was preparing to bake bread," Charlie said. She could see that Jesse's brothers and their wives approved of Harvey's suggestion, but she also noticed Sheila and her mother giving her looks that dared her to sit at the same table with them. "I already had my dinner," she said lamely.

"Then you can join us for dessert," Harvey stated. "I don't want to hear any more excuses. Dinner is getting cold, and the twins are about to droop. Sit beside Jesse," he said, pointing at the empty seat beside his brother. Jesse pulled the chair out, but Charlie's feet refused to move.

Jesse noticed that Charlie seemed frozen where she stood, so he rose from his place and took her elbow, then led her to the table. Charlie could barely eat, and she kept her head down as she nibbled on the peach Jesse had placed on her plate. As soon as it was possible to leave the table, she excused herself, shot up and rushed back to the kitchen. She knew that she would get it from Aunt Vero and her daughter as soon as they had the chance to talk to her.

HERE COMES TROUBLE

Charlie clenched her fists and willed herself to calm down. Never had she been treated with such disdain before. Even Aunt Lena and her household had treated her with cold indifference and the occasional snide remarks at most, but never such blatant spite.

"Wipe it up now, will you," Sheila said even as she spilled more coffee on the clean floor. Charlie had spent the morning scrubbing the kitchen floor and now this person was messing it up, pouring coffee and then stepping into the spill and walking around the kitchen. Marks were strewn all over the place and the floor looked like it hadn't been cleaned in years. "You need to remember that you're nothing but a servant in this house and should know your place. How dare you think that you can sit at the table with the masters of this house? My cousins' wives must be horrified to think that you're placing yourself at the same level with them. Why did you insist on sitting down to dinner with us when you're not supposed to? Who taught you manners? And stop looking at me like that or I'll slap you."

Charlie raised her eyes and looked straight at Sheila. "I dare you to try that," her voice was low and menacing. "And see what will happen to you."

"How dare you talk to me like that? I'll tell Harvey, and you can be sure that you've landed yourself in trouble. Such insolence!"

Charlie realized that the more she continued standing in Sheila's presence, the more likely it was that they would end up exchanging words, if not blows. She respected her masters and their wives too much to descend into such disrespectful behavior.

"What's going on in here?" Sophie walked into the tension-filled kitchen and saw the spillage on the floor. She also saw the dirt marks all over and frowned. "Charlie, the kitchen is always spic and span. What's going on here?"

"I told this person..."

"Sheila," Sophie interrupted her cousin by marriage, "This is Charlotte, and it's disrespectful to speak of her in such a tone and in my presence."

"She's nothing but a servant," the young woman said.

"That still doesn't give you the right to speak to her as if you're addressing a child. What's going on?"

"Sophie, it's all right," Charlie didn't want her cousin getting into a fighting match with her cousin-in-law. She cleaned up the mess on the floor and moved to the sink to wash the dishes that were there. It was two days since Aunt Vero and Sheila had arrived, and to Charlie these were trying times indeed.

The two women had come in and tried to put Lauren, Glenda, and Sophie down while implying that their husbands had married beneath them. The three men, Walter, Joe and George, respective husbands of the three had risen up strongly in their wives' defense.

"Touch my wife, touch my life," Walter had growled at his aunt and cousin.

The other two had been more subtle, but the message had been clear that they wouldn't stand for anyone disrespecting their wives.

Charlie knew that the two women were frustrated and looking for someone to vent their anger on. Well, she was going to do all she could to avoid any kind of trouble.

"Insofar as is dependent on me," she quoted under her breath, *"I'll do all I can to live at peace with every man, woman, and child in this house."*

She watched as Sophie herded Sheila out and breathed a sigh of relief. She heard heavy footsteps coming down the hallway, and when she turned around, she saw that it was Jesse.

"Good morning, Charlie," he smiled at her, and she blushed. This man's presence was enough to make the butterflies in her stomach flutter as if they wanted to burst out and fly into the air.

"Good morning, Mr. Jesse," she responded. "Breakfast will soon be ready. I'm sorry for the delay."

"Charlie, don't vex yourself. I came to see if you need any help from me," he said.

"Not today, Sir," she waved a hand at the pots on the stove. "I have everything under control, and all I need to do is serve. I was just waiting for everyone to wake up so I can carry the food to the dining table."

"Oh, Charlie! Would you stop with all this Sir and Mister nonsense? My name is Jesse, and you need to learn how to use it."

"Jesse, my dear boy, do you think it's wise to have the servants calling you by name?" Aunt Vero walked into the kitchen. "Even the Bible forbids it."

"Really?" Jesse gave his mother's sister a sardonic smile.

"Yes, Jesse. The Bible says that if you're in the habit of giving your servant everything, one day she will take over all that you own. Servants need to always know their places in their masters' houses," and she glared at Charlie as she spoke those words. "We're waiting for you to serve breakfast, and here you are just dallying around as if you have nothing to do. Hop to it, girl!"

"Yes, Ma'am."

Jesse scowled at his aunt's tone, and as soon as she left the kitchen, he turned to Charlie. "Why do you allow her to talk to you like that?"

Charlie merely shrugged, "Really, it's nothing."

"I don't like the way my aunt and cousin speak to you, Charlie. I'm sorry about the way they have no respect for you."

Charlie smiled, "Jesse, please don't think anything about it."

Jesse observed her and realized that she was used to being put down and treated badly. It wasn't right, and Jesse determined that such would never happen under their roof.

~

JESSE WAS HELPING Charlie prepare dinner when Aunt Vero walked into the kitchen. Charlie had gone to the garden to get some coriander leaves to garnish the stew and Jesse was making sure the thick bean soup didn't stick to the bottom of the pot, hence his stirring it.

"Jesse Reuben Chester, what do you think you're doing?" Aunt Vero looked around. "Where is that girl? How dare she shirk from doing her household duties and expect you as her master to do them? What is this world coming to? Servants become masters and masters turn into servants."

"Aunt Vera, please lower your voice," Jesse said as he carried on stirring the stew in the pot. "I've been cooking all my life and you know it. What's the difference now?"

"Jesse that's a woman's work or better still, the maid is supposed to do it."

Jesse sighed. His aunt would never change. Once a snob, he thought, always a snob. He wanted her gone from the house because her presence was creating problems that he didn't like. She seemed to really have it in for Charlie and was always looking for ways to humiliate her.

Charlie walked into the kitchen, and Aunt Vero turned on her. "Where have you been?" Aunt Vero snapped. "You're an incompetent person, and if it was up to me, I'd make sure that you leave my house at once."

"Aunt Vero, that's quite enough!"

"No Jesse, this girl has to be put in her right place or else she'll begin to think that she's part of this family when she's nothing but a servant." She turned to Charlie, "I'm talking, and you're just standing there staring at me as if you don't have any sense in the brain God gave you."

Charlie had had enough, and she felt pain and anger welling up within her. She'd done nothing to warrant such an attack from this woman who didn't even know her.

"I've done nothing wrong, but you won't stop coming at me and trying to humiliate me all the time," she faced Aunt Vero, who took a step backwards at the rage she saw on Charlie's face. "What do you want from me? Do you want me to prostrate myself before you so you can walk all over my back because I'm just a servant in this house?" She placed the bunch of freshly picked coriander on the kitchen counter and turned to walk out of the house again.

"Where do you think you're going?"

Charlie didn't even turn around nor answer. She left through the back door and made it as far as the corral before giving in to her tears; she slumped against the railing and cried.

All the pain she'd carried through the years came gushing out, and she wept for all her lost years without love and acceptance. Even as she cried, she was careful not to startle the ponies which were idling in the corral.

"I can't take any more of this," she put her head on her arms and cried. "Why do people see the need to always pick on me even when I haven't provoked them in any way? Am I such a repulsive human being that people find it so easy to hate me?"

She had no idea that someone was watching her and did so for a long time, until she left the corral. Harvey's lips tightened as he made sure the weeping woman didn't see him. He slipped to the back of the stable and forced himself to calm down. He knew that Charlie was crying because of his aunt and cousin. Something had to be done about those two.

SHE DOESN'T BELONG

"They're right," Charlie shivered in misery as she fed the dogs. "I don't belong in this rich world. It's like Aunt Lena's house all over again," then she laughed softly. "But at least I get paid in this place."

She actually felt better after the bout of weeping at the corral, but she was avoiding returning back to the house because her face was puffed up and her eyes were red and swollen. She recalled Sophie once telling her that she should never show her foes that she was hurt by their words.

"Always walk away if you feel that you're about to break down and weep before your foes. Don't make them feel that they have any power or control over you."

She felt a hand on her shoulder and nearly cried out. It was Jesse.

"I don't like seeing you like this," he said. "Don't take what my aunt says to heart. She can't do anything other than just talk. You have me, and I'll never let anyone hurt you in any way, Charlie."

"You can't be here with me," Charlie said, looking around as if she was afraid to be seen with him. "I don't need any more trouble from your relatives, please just leave me alone."

"Charlie, you don't mean that," he drew closer and crouched beside her. He touched her cheek and she pulled away. "Why are you so blind?"

"I don't understand."

"Charlie, you've been pushing me away, when all I want is to show you that I have very strong feelings for you."

"You have feelings for me?" Charlie stared at Jesse with wide eyes. "What are you talking about?"

"That I'm falling in love with you," Jesse said and was startled when Charlie shot to her feet.

"Don't say that!" She put her hands over her ears. "You don't know what you're saying. How can a person like you say that to me?"

"Why shouldn't I say whatever is in my heart?"

"Because it's not true. Your kind only likes to play with people's emotions. Surely, a wealthy man like you can

73

never consider a lowly maidservant such as myself. The kind of woman you should be saying that to is like your cousin in there," she said and walked away.

Charlie was about to open the kitchen door and walk in when she heard Harvey's cold voice.

"I've been trying so hard not to get involved in this matter, but you're taking matters too far, Aunt Vero. Charlie is an important member of this family, and I won't have anyone disrespecting her in any way. I was coming to the house to get some water when I heard you speaking to Charlie in a very disrespectful way. You crossed the line, and I want you to apologize to Charlie as soon as she comes back into the house."

"I'm sorry Harvey, I didn't know that Charlotte would take offense so easily. I didn't mean any harm by it."

"None of your words to Charlie have been kind, and I don't want a repeat of such words again. Am I understood? And that goes for you too, Sheila."

"We've heard you," Aunt Vero said.

Charlie refused to join the family at the dinner table that evening even when Harvey asked her to do so. Aunt Vero and Sheila pretended to add their voices to those persuading Charlie to sit with them.

"Charlotte, my nephew Harvey made me understand that

I'd offended you at lunch time. Please forgive me and know that I didn't intend to do so."

Charlie merely gave her a slight nod but said nothing.

"Please join us," Sheila said with false brightness. "You're family after all, and from today my mother and I will treat and respect you as such."

"That's good Sheila and thank you," Harvey said. "Charlie, it's all right, you can return to the kitchen and carry on with whatever you were doing."

"Thank you, Sir."

DON'T TOUCH MY LOVE

Sleep proved impossible for Jesse. He gave up trying long before dawn, and instead found himself in the milking shed, cleaning it up. His jaw clenched and unclenched as he thought about what Charlie had been silently enduring at the hands of his aunt and cousin. But for Harvey's intervention, Jesse would have driven the two women off the ranch without a single moment's hesitation.

Because of his aunt, any strides Jesse had made toward Charlie had been lost. Now she thought all wealthy people were bad. Not that he even blamed her because Sophie had revealed a lot about Charlie's background. He needed to find a way of making Charlie see that he was different. He was in love with her and like Harvey had told him, this time his heart knew that it was real.

But to be fair, Aunt Vero and Sheila had promised to change and treat Charlie as part of the family.

"We shall see," Jesse murmured as his eyes shut in sleep.

∼

CHARLIE WAS surprised when she found Aunt Vero and Sheila in the kitchen early the next morning. She immediately wanted to turn around and disappear, but the older woman called her back.

"Charlie, don't run away from us; we don't bite," the smile was smooth, but Charlie was wary, feeling that it wasn't sincere. She gave the older woman a tight smile of her own.

"My nephew brought it to my attention that my daughter and I have offended you. Please forgive us. More than anything I want you to feel that this is your home. Henceforth, Sheila and I will be helping you with the house chores. We'll treat you like a member of this family because that's what Harvey expects us to do."

Charlie bowed her head and listened. Everything Aunt Vero was saying sounded true but there was something deep within Charlie's heart that rejected the words. She didn't think they were sincere at all.

"*Faithful are the wounds of a friend, but the kisses of an enemy are deceitful,*" Charlie thought to herself. She was sure

Aunt Vero was doing all this because her nephews were around the house, as were their wives. And she was right!

As soon as breakfast was over. Lauren, Glenda, and Sophie took the twins and went over to visit Aunt Zippy. The elderly woman wasn't feeling well, and Sophie was going to check on her while the others were to clean her house and prepare her meals for the day.

Once the house was silent and Charlie was done cleaning and tidying up the rooms, she returned to the kitchen to begin lunch preparations. Aunt Vero and Sheila walked in a few minutes after her. Their countenances toward her were anything but friendly, and Charlie braced herself for the worst.

"I felt like gagging when I was apologizing to you last evening because Harvey expected it of me," Sheila hissed at Charlie. "You think we're here to make things easy for you?" She laughed sarcastically. "That's the last thing we'll ever think of doing."

"I don't know why my nephews treat you as though you're a part of this family, yet you're not. Do you know what you are, Charlotte? An imposter, a charlatan and you don't deserve to be in this house."

With all that was going on, Charlie held her peace.

∼

Georgε Chester woke up feeling a little under the weather, but because he didn't want his lovely wife finding out that he was feeling poorly, he forced himself to look all right.

After breakfast he watched Sophie and her sisters-in-law leaving to visit Aunt Zippy at her cottage and they took the twins with them.

George then retired to his bedroom to rest for a while. He told himself that as soon as he felt better, he would join his brothers out on the range. He lay on his bed and dozed off.

Then suddenly he was woken up by raised voices.

"What now?" He groaned inwardly. His aunt's voice was the loudest and Sheila's matched it. At first, he thought that mother and daughter were having a spate. But as he listened keenly, he realized that the attack was directed at someone else.

"Charlie!" He thought. The poor woman had been having it rough with his aunt and cousin until Harvey's intervention. George frowned as he heard the continuous insults toward Charlie. He'd thought that the whole conflict had been resolved last night but apparently things were even worse now.

As George listened to the scolding and berating, he realized that his aunt and cousin had only been

79

pretending to change. He got out of bed and tiptoed to the door so he could clearly hear whatever was going on.

"You're not a member of this family and can never be," Aunt Vero was saying. "Because of you, my nephews now think that I'm a bad person. Is it wrong for me as their mother's sister to run this home for them? I'm like a mother to my sister's sons, so whatever goes on under this roof is of much concern to me. Now, I really don't think you're the kind of person who should be serving in this house. You're nothing but a disgrace to women, and I want you gone from here so I can find a better cook for my nephews."

"Yes, you must leave this house at once," Sheila piped. "Or else you'll see what we'll do to you. You're not our kind and can never be, so don't even imagine that my cousins will defend you against my mother. They love her too much and will do anything she asks them to."

"Don't look at me like that," Aunt Vero hissed. "The best way to get rid of you is to make you look bad before my nephews, like you've done to me. I know just what to do, and believe me, my nephews will not just chase you away, they'll drive you out with nothing and you can go out there where you belong."

"Mama, it's so easy to get rid of this kind of woman. I'll put my jewelry in her room and then tell my cousins that she stole it. I don't think my cousins will want to continue harboring a thief under their roof."

George was shocked, and he'd heard enough. Whatever else they said after that didn't matter. He'd heard enough to implicate them, and he returned to his bedroom to ponder over what he'd just heard.

∽

Charlie knew that there was no way she could defend herself against the accusations leveled against her, especially when Sheila's jewelry was found in one of the drawers of her bedside table. Harvey had summoned her just as she was getting ready to serve dinner. Everyone listened in stunned silence as Aunt Vero told of seeing Charlie sneaking out of their room when they were out on the lawn.

"I thought she'd gone in there to clean the room but then Sheila realized that the necklace and bracelet she wanted to wear were gone. We wanted to go to town this afternoon, but my poor child couldn't find her jewelry and was so distraught. It was a special gift from her father for her birthday this year and she was so sad when she thought she'd lost it."

"Wait!" George said when Sheila made a show of weeping at the loss of her jewelry and relief that it had all been found.

"What is it, George? This is a very serious issue now."

"I know that, Harvey, but you've got it all wrong. Charlie is innocent of the accusations against her."

"George, our cousin's missing jewelry was found in her room. How do you explain that?"

George laughed and gave his aunt and cousin a disgusted look. "This morning when you all left, Aunt Vero and Cousin Sheila must have thought that we were all gone from the house," he saw how startled the two women were. "Yes, I was feeling a little under the weather and so I stayed behind to rest. I heard these two plotting on how they would get rid of Charlie. It was Sheila herself who came up with the idea of putting her jewelry in Charlie's room, then pretending that it had been stolen. A search would then reveal that the jewelry was in Charlie's room."

"What?" Harvey's eyes turned chilly as they settled on his relatives. "Is that true?"

Aunt Vero and Sheila looked down.

"Harvey," George went on. "That's exactly what our aunt and cousin did. They want Charlie gone from this house and are prepared to do whatever it takes."

"Not happening," Jesse growled.

"And that's not all. They both told Charlie to her face that she's not a member of this family and can never be. Can you believe their audacity?" George looked disgusted and Charlie wanted to smile.

Suddenly the hunters had become the hunted and she recalled the verse in Psalm one hundred and twenty-four that said, '*Our soul is escaped as a bird out of the snare of the fowlers; The snare is broken, and we are escaped.*'

The Lord had fought for her, and she was now vindicated, and she couldn't help the smile that spread across her lips. She noticed that Jesse was glaring at his relatives as if he wanted to pick them up and cast them out of the house.

MARCHING ORDERS

"Aunt Veronica, you had no right to say such things to Charlie, and certainly not under our roof," Harvey's voice was very cold.

Jesse was surprised that his aunt didn't even look apologetic. There was a smug and self-righteous look on her face.

"I have every right to send this woman out of this house. Your mother was my elder sister, and in her absence, I have to protect you from the wrong kind of women. What kind of aunt would I be if I allowed just anybody to live in my nephews' house?"

"Who is the wrong kind of woman?" Jesse snapped.

"From women who will only come around you because of your wealth and those who don't know their place…"

"With the remaining respect that I have for you, Aunt Vero," Sophie cut her off, "Please be careful of the next words that leave your lips. The only reason I'm being this cordial with you is because of my husband. But just know this, you and Sheila are no longer welcome in this house. You need to leave."

Aunt Vero's façade faded, and she looked slightly shaken. "Harvey, you can't let this woman talk to me like that."

"But it was all right for you to talk to Charlie very disrespectfully? My mother was your sister, and she may have allowed you certain liberties while she was here. But I'm the head of this house now, and everyone who lives with or works for me, comes under my protection. I won't let you disrespect Charlie or any of my other sisters-in-law. Walter will get the carriage ready and drive the two of you to the train station early tomorrow morning."

"Cousin Harvey, how can you choose a stranger over your family?" Sheila pouted. "Don't you know that family always comes first?"

Jesse scoffed at her, "Family will only come first when there's respect for everyone in it. You've acted so badly, and I'm with Sophie when I say that you need to leave."

Harvey nodded, "I've chosen Charlie because she isn't just the housekeeper," and as he spoke his eyes went to Jesse who saw the approval in them. "Charlie is family. The first train tomorrow morning leaves by seven and you need to be on it."

Aunt Vero sniffed, "Your mother would never have treated us so badly."

"It's sad that you're supposed to be our counselor and advisor, yet you've been nothing but trouble since your arrival. You never even let us know that you were coming, but suddenly showed up here—and not in peace." Harvey said. "My brothers and I don't want to disrespect you because you're still an important member of our family. But respect goes both ways, Aunt Vero. If you respect us and our household, then we'll accord you the same."

"I still don't believe that you would choose a stranger over your family, Cousin Harvey."

Jesse rose to his feet, "That's where you're wrong, Cousin Sheila. Charlie isn't a stranger but the woman I'm going to marry."

The two women gaped at him with their mouths wide open.

Sophie rose to her feet, "I want Aunt Vero and Cousin Sheila gone by tomorrow morning. I won't have anyone disrespecting and mistreating my beloved cousin. Charlie has been through so much and I won't stand by and see anyone make her life painful all over again."

"My love," George held his wife's hand. "Let it be. Harvey is dealing with the issue."

"Just as long as it becomes clear that Aunt Vero and Cousin Sheila are leaving tomorrow. I'm not saying that they can't visit ever again. It's just that right now there's much pain and anger, and it won't be good for us to remain under the same roof."

Charlie watched all the goings on in silence, not believing that a powerful and wealthy family like the Chesters would stand up for her. She'd expected them to have taken the side of their relatives.

What surprised her more was when Jesse stood up and made his declaration. Or perhaps he'd been speaking in jest, so he could put his relatives in their place. She looked at his face, no, he didn't look like he was speaking in jest.

Then he smiled at her, and she felt her insides melting. He meant every word he'd said, and his eyes told her so.

∼

CHARLIE COULDN'T BELIEVE the silence that reigned in the house once the meeting broke up. Aunt Vero and Sheila remained closeted in their bedrooms, and no one bothered about them.

Still, Charlie prepared enough food and left it on the stove because she knew the two women would eventually get hungry. Let it never be said that she left anyone hungry in the house.

"What are you still doing in the kitchen at this time?" Jesse walked in and found Charlie seated at the kitchen table. She was shelling some walnuts. "It's late and you should be in bed right now."

"I'll soon go but I was preparing something for Aunt Vero and Cousin Sheila to eat. They haven't had their dinner, and I don't want them to go to bed hungry."

"You're an exceptional woman, Charlie. And you have such a large heart of gold. Despite all they did to you, here you are still taking good care of them."

Charlie merely shrugged, "It's the right thing to do. Do you want anything to eat or drink?" She rose from the chair. "I was just making some chocolate."

"I'll take some if you'll join me."

"Very well then."

Jesse couldn't help staring at Charlie. She was a strong woman and yet still so tender, and all he wanted was to protect and keep her safe.

"Why are you staring at me like that?" Charlie asked shyly.

"Because you're so beautiful, and all I want to do is to look at you day and night, Charlie," Jesse rose from his seat and knelt before her. "I know that you've been through so much and are afraid of 'my kind' as you call us. But here I am, baring my heart to you. I've never felt this way about any other woman before, not even those two that I thought I was in love with before. Charlie, being around you gives me so much peace, and I never want to be far from you." He shook his head. "I wake up wanting to see you, and I go to bed thinking about you, Charlie. Sometimes I fear that I might be dreaming. Twice before I thought myself to be in love, but it wasn't anything close to what I feel for you right now." He took her right hand and placed it over his heart. "Charlie, I want you to take my heart and keep it safe for me."

"Oh, Jesse!" Charlie whispered.

"And this," he pulled a ring out of his pocket. "This is a very special ring that was given to me by my grandmother for the woman who holds my heart forever. She said that I should never give it to just anybody but only to that one special woman in my life. Charlie, you're that woman and it's an honor to my grandmother for you to wear this ring."

"I don't know what to say," Charlie felt like crying but they were tears of happiness.

"Please don't say anything. All I want is for you to give me your heart, and I promise that I'll cherish it forever. I'll love you forever and insofar as is in my power, I'll always protect you. Will you accept my ring and be my wife?"

"Yes," Charlie nodded happily.

"We'll get married as soon as I inform our pastor," Jesse said. "You can be sure that this week won't end before you become my blushing bride."

∼

CHARLIE WAS surprised when before sunrise the next day, the whole family was awake. She quickly prepared coffee and placed it on the dining table, but no one took it just yet. Last evening's activities were fresh in her mind, and she looked at her finger, which felt heavy. She'd never won a ring before, and the diamonds glittered merrily, causing her to smile.

She was about to make pancakes when she heard heavy trunks being dragged down the hallway, and curious, she went to the door to peep.

"Aunt Vero, these are mother's clothes, shoes and hats, and I know she would want you to have them," Harvey told his aunt. "I'd been thinking of a way to have them sent to you, but you saved me the journey."

Charlie expected the woman to show some appreciation and was surprised when she didn't. Instead, Aunt Vero made some more demands.

"You know that I deserve to have my sister's jewelry. I don't know why you still refuse to hand it over to me."

"We won't go over that again, Aunt Vero," Harvey's voice turned cold. "In fact, because of your ingratitude, you can leave without my mother's clothes and other accessories. We'll donate them to charity because those people will at least appreciate the gifts."

"No," the woman said hastily. "We'll take them. But what about the money I asked for?"

"Listen to me, Aunt Vero. My uncle works hard to provide a good life for you and Sheila. If you lived within your means you wouldn't have to get into debt and come asking for money. I heard you when you told me that you got money from a shylock. Give me the name of the person who lent you money and is bothering you and I'll have my lawyer look him up and settle him."

"Harvey, I don't want the man to think that I'm broadcasting him to the world. He might feel very bad, and I wouldn't want to offend him."

"I'm not the world and I doubt that any shylock would feel bad about being paid his money. You said you owed him six thousand dollars, right? Well, write down his name and address and I'll settle him one way or the other. But next time I won't be so kind."

Jesse laughed when his aunt and cousin went without leaving behind the shylock's details. "I had a feeling that Aunt Vero was lying just to get some money from you, Harvey."

Harvey smiled, "I sent a telegram to our uncle two days ago, and he replied yesterday. He told me that Sheila had gotten involved with a married man, and when the wife found out, things became rather ugly. To escape the shame and embarrassment, Aunt Vero decided to come to Beaverhead until the fire had died down. I'm sure she wanted six thousand dollars so she and Sheila could disappear for a long while. Uncle told me to throw them out of the house and let them return to face the music. Well, I wouldn't have done it if they'd been kind and nice to Charlie. As it is, let them go and deal with their issues."

"She was so insistent about Mama's jewelry," Walter said. "Maybe Mama wanted her to have it."

"No, and you all know it. That jewelry is in a safety deposit box and will stay there until the right time," Jesse said. "All I can say for now is good riddance and I hope they don't return any time soon."

THE GIRL IS MINE

*J*esse had never considered himself to be a nervous man. He was used to tackling huge bulls and large stallions; he'd dealt with coyotes, bears and even rogue Indians who wanted to steal their sheep. He'd also looked down the barrel of a rustler's gun once and subdued the man. But watching Charlie walking toward him, he found himself shifting from one foot to the other. He was very nervous and felt fire in the pit of his belly. Nothing had ever mattered to him or been so important as this moment.

Charlie stopped a few feet from Jesse, and shyness coupled with nervousness took over. It was their wedding day, and because their church building was being renovated, the ceremony was taking place at their homestead.

Charlie couldn't believe how many people had turned up for the wedding, even though they'd announced it just two days ago. Her heart was beating as if it wanted to jump right out of her chest as she looked at the face of the man she loved so deeply.

"And yet another Chester gets struck down by the arrow of love," George snickered from the side and there were hoots of laughter all around.

Jesse ignored the good-natured teasing he was getting from his brothers because his eyes were only for the woman who stood shyly before him.

"Charlie, you passed every test for a bride that I've been praying for. Over the weeks as I've watched you, I've seen in you the kindest and most humble person I know. You came into my life when I had despaired of finding a woman who would truly love me for me and not for what I have. In you I've found my heart and my home, and I'll love you for the rest of my life."

"Jesse, each time I see you I feel as if my heart is about to skip a beat," Charlie said softly so he was the only one who could hear. "You fill my heart with so much happiness that I can't believe that this is actually me."

"My darling."

"Jesse, I love you so much and will love you for the rest of my life too."

And everyone said amen.

THANK YOU FOR CHOOSING A PUREREAD BOOK!

We hope you enjoyed the story, and as a way to thank you for choosing PureRead we'd like to send you this free Western trilogy, and other fun reader rewards...

Click here to claim your free Historical Western trilogy...
https://pureread.com/western

Thanks again for reading.
See you soon!

OTHER BOOKS IN THIS SERIES

If you loved this story why not continue straight away with other books in the series?

Read them all...

Unbroken Promises

Safe in His Western Arms

Dawn at Moonbeam Ranch

Healing the Cowboy's Heart

OUR GIFT TO YOU

AS A WAY TO SAY THANK YOU WE WOULD LOVE TO SEND YOU THIS BEAUTIFUL TRILOGY FREE OF CHARGE.

Our Reader List is 100% FREE

Click here to claim your free Historical Western trilogy...
https://pureread.com/western

At PureRead we publish books you can trust. Great tales without smut or swearing, but with all of the mystery and romance you expect from a great story.

Be the first to know when we release new books, take part in our fun competitions, and get surprise free books in your inbox by signing up to our Reader list.

As a thank you you'll receive this exclusive Western trilogy - a beautiful collection available only to our subscribers...

Click here to claim your free Historical Western trilogy...

https://pureread.com/western

Made in United States
Troutdale, OR
08/17/2025